SALLY SMALL

Library of Congress Cataloging-in-Publication Data

Smith-Moore, J. J., 1955-
  Sally Small.

  Summary: Sally learns that good things come in
small packages, including herself, after her wish to
be tall is granted.
  [1. Size—Fiction. 2. Stories in rhyme] I. Title.
PZ8.3.S6716Sal 1989 [E]   88-31764
ISBN 0-8431-2360-5

Copyright © 1988 by J.J. Smith-Moore
Published by Price Stern Sloan, Inc.
360 North La Cienega Boulevard, Los Angeles, California 90048

ISBN: 0-8431-2360-5

SALLY SMALL

by J.J. Smith-Moore

PRICE STERN SLOAN

Los Angeles

To my cousin,
Sally M. Olin,
Who stands tall, tall, tall,
With her love for all!

J.J. S.M.

Sally was unusually small
And this did not make her happy . . .
At all!

Her friends at school and home
Were tall,

Taller than our Sally Small.

Even at the local zoo,
The animals were bigger too!

Everywhere that Sally went,
She found height—
But not content.

So late at night,
When in her bed,
She would pray
Above her head . . .

"The wish I ask
Is simply this—
Grant the tallness
That I miss!
I do try
Not to ask for much,
But you make things grow and such,
So here I am, your Sally Small,
Once again,
Wishing to be tall."

Then dear Sally went to sleep,
With thoughts of inches at her feet.

Soon all at once,

In a slow sway,

Her small bed started to give way!

When she awoke
From her fitful sleep
She had grown to fourteen feet!

As she started to sit up,
She soon was twenty-two feet up!

Above the trees
She rose up high,
High, high up into the sky!

Past the clouds,
The moon and stars,
Until she was as tall as Mars!

Sally called,
"Hello! hello!"
But no one heard her
Down below.
She looked around
And soon she found
That no one was taller
Than her very own crown.

And this did not make her happy
At all,
Because now
She . . . missed . . . being . . . small.

She looked to the star,
Above on her right,
And wished with all her big, tall might:

"I want to be small again,
Little, like when the day began.
I just hadn't known
I'd be *so* overgrown.
I've made a mistake,
Oh, how my heart aches!

"I miss my small head
And my tiny little bed.
No more do I want to be tall.
I'm much better small.
Small, small, looking up at it all!
Things would be much better, then,
The way they were, way back when."

Then Sally awoke
In her very small bed
And she looked out her window
Above her little head.

She saw the clouds,
The moon and stars,
And thought a bit about quiet Mars.

Eventually, she fell
Back to sleep,
This time without making
One . . . little . . . peep.

And Sally found,
As she looked around,
That to be small

Is not much different
Than being tall.

That happiness, after all,
Is most important,
Not whether you are small or tall.

So that's the story
Of our Sally Small,
Whose dreams have changed
Of wishing to be tall . . .

That's All!